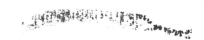

MALL OUT OF LUCK

AT THE MALL HOLIDAY STANDALONE NOVELLA

SARAH ROBINSON

D1377601

CHAPTER ONE

NELL

DID YOU SEE THIS?

Nell James read the text message that popped up on her phone followed by a link to a local blog article. Her best friend, Mara Hart, spent way too much time on social media and was always the first one to send her breaking news—or post cute Instagram pictures of her and her husband Val doing cute, romantic things around town. Not that Nell wasn't happy for her—she was—but with Valentine's Day only a few weeks behind her, it had become painfully obvious how single she still was.

She pulled the impact goggles off her face and placed them next to the beaker she'd just been working with before scanning the article attached to the link.

Throwback Jack's Under New Ownership— Launch on March 17, 2022.

What! Nell texted Mara back immediately upon seeing the title. *TJ closed?*

She'd been going to Throwback Jack's for over five years now and was part of a local darts league that always practiced there. Being a vaccine scientist during the day meant that she needed time to unwind in the evening and on weekends, and playing darts with other thirty-year-olds in a recreational league had been a big source of that for her lately. Her current efforts at her job on the Sandfly Fever Sicilian Virus vaccine project were at a standstill, and she'd been going out after work more often than ever before.

Not that she was about to advertise that to her colleagues or invite them to join her.

Being a woman in the field of STEM (Science, Technology, Engineering, and Mathematics) was hard enough, but being a former-foster-child, current-lesbian in STEM? The misogyny deck had been stacked against her from day one. She'd had to prove herself twice as competent as the men on her team just to earn the same level of respect—and even that still meant she'd get the occasional ask to *be a doll and grab me a coffee, won't you?*

Ugh. The reminder made her stomach lurch with patriarchal resentment. She made a mental note to call her adopted brother, Dash—also a former-foster kid—and tell him about the latest office antics with Mr. Staffi down the hall from her where he'd formally written human resources to complain about free tampons in the women's room and nothing free in the men's room. Dash lived on the other side of the country with his little, happy family now, but he still knew how to throw in a well-timed joke that made her feel better when she was feeling ragey towards "the man."

Despite those obstacles in her career path, she'd managed to work her way up to one of the top positions in her organization and was a leading researcher on this current vaccine project. Simply put, she was proud of all she'd accomplished.

No, they're open now. Mara responded to her previous text message. *The soft start was yesterday, I guess. Big launch on St. Patty's Day. We should go! I bet Val can close the store for a day or get someone to cover. You can be our third wheel!*

Nell frowned but felt a little relief that at least the bar was still open—only to have that quickly disappear at the thought of being yet another third wheel to her friend's happy love story. She wondered why she hadn't heard anything from the darts league, and if that meant that things were changing for the upcoming Pot O' Gold St. Patrick's Day tournament that Throwback Jack's used to host every year.

Maybe I should go tonight and find out? She clicked back onto the link and read the article further.

It's no secret that Throwback Jack's has been struggling over the last few years to appeal to a younger audience, so when news came that ownership had changed, no one here at Michigan Mishigas was surprised. But when we learned who the new owner was though? Things became interesting, to say the least.

Saoirse (pronounced Sur-Sha) Walsh hails from a town of less than five hundred people in Nebraska—and she's already left three of them at the altar. Now she's come to Yule Heights, Michigan with plans to launch a bar named The Lucky Leprechaun right where Throwback Jack's used to be. This writer thinks The Unlucky Leprechaun might be a better fitting name at this point!

She chuckled lightly at the blogger's commentary, though she couldn't imagine the focal point of the piece would feel the same way if she read it. She clicked the photograph included with the article and pulled up a picture of a woman with bright red hair and dark green eyes —almost emerald—standing behind a bar with a big smile on her face that looked like she was ready to take on the world. Too bad there was a cut-out photo in the bottom right that was three different engagement photo shoots—all different partners with Saoirse, including two men and one woman, all obscured to hide the almost-spouses faces for (she assumed) privacy reasons. The caption under the photo read: "I almost do!"

Man, they're really taking this poor girl's back story and running with it.

Nell opened up her text messages to Mara again and sent back a quick laughing face emoji. *Oh my God, the byline though.*

Right? They don't have high hopes for that place, Mara responded seconds later.

She's hot though, Nell replied.

She clicked over to the woman's photo again, examining her a moment longer. She really was beautiful, and there was something freeing about already knowing Saoirse was interested in women before having even met her. It wasn't that Yule Heights was super conservative, but it was very small. There were maybe four lesbians who lived in this town that were open and out, and maybe twice that number of gay men. If she wanted a date, she had to set her Tinder settings to pretty far out because she'd learned quickly that mucking around in her own town was a recipe for disaster. And she wasn't just saying that because the last woman she dated was a chef at the only fancy restaurant in town and now that place was off limits to her for the rest of time. She already missed their garlic bread.

"Nell?" Mr. Staffi popped his head in her laboratory

door. His nose wrinkled and he squinted his eyes at her. "Is that smell coming from in here?"

She frowned and sniffed the air. Nothing was striking her as out of the ordinary, and she glanced at the chemicals she was working with—all of which were odorless. "No, not me."

"You know, you *could* bring in some deodorizer." Mr. Staffi lifted his nose in the air just enough to be looking down at her—his favorite way of viewing the world. "We don't provide it, but most scientists bring their own if they know they're going to be working with such pungent smells."

Nell cleared her throat and walked over to the doorway where he was standing. In a loud, exaggerated sound, she sniffed the air. "I don't know, Mr. Staffi. That doesn't smell like my aluminum hydroxide. It *does*, however, smell like...did you have tuna for lunch, Mr. Staffi?"

His face tinged a darker shade of his normal red. "Well, yes. I did. But that was yesterday."

"I think that's it." She pushed back on her heels and crossed her arms over her chest. "You've got the tuna mouth."

So dark red, his face was nearly purple. "I will have you know that I brush my teeth every night and morning."

"But did you scrape your tongue?" She used a light-hearted lilt in her voice now, enjoying that she was driving him nuts. Served him right. Dealing with him day in and day out in the office next door was exhausting. "That's what people always forget. The smell is stuck to your tongue. It's the Tuna Tongue. And I'm so sorry to say, but it's not curable."

His nostrils flared and he rolled his eyes. "I'm reporting

this to Human Resources." He turned on his heels and stomped down the hallway. "This office smells."

Nell stuck her head out the door, watching him walk away and unable to resist one final quip. "Ask for Susie. She has my number on speed dial!"

She laughed as she walked back into her office and glanced at the clock. It was already well into the evening hours, and she would have been off hours ago if she hadn't become wrapped up in this project she was working on. *Oh, well.* Now seemed like as good a time as any to call it quits for the day and maybe give this new bar a try on her way home.

And maybe meet a new woman...

CHAPTER TWO

SAOIRSE

Saoirse Walsh swiped her phone screen, closing out the article she'd just received a Google Alert on—she needed to disable that notification permanently. Heck, she wasn't sure why she hadn't already. Every time something was posted about her online, it was about one—or all three—of her weddings. Or, more accurately, her almost-weddings. Canceled weddings? Whatever the appropriate terminology, it was her least favorite topic of all time.

"Boss, do you need these up front?" An older gentleman stuck his head through the swinging door that separated the kitchen and back storage room from the front of the bar. In his surprisingly muscular arms was a rack of glasses that he had, presumably, just washed.

"Under there, Donner. Thanks." She pointed to an open slot under the bar where the rack could slide right in. "Hey, do you have any ideas for the launch party? You're from here, right? Maybe there's something the local folks are really into? Some type of giveaway or drink?"

The man lifted one bushy eyebrow after shoving the rack into the bar. He'd told her that he only agreed to take this job because his usual seasonal work lasted from October to December and then he needed to fill the rest of his year. "Do I look like a publicist? Hire someone who knows that kind of stuff. Event planner or whatever. Just leave me in charge of the stock room and kitchen."

"I met with a public relations manager yesterday who has been really helpful," she replied. She did trust the manager and felt like she knew what she was doing, but still...she was nervous about the entire thing. This launch had to go perfectly if she wanted her reputation here in town to be anything other than the runaway bride.

"Hey, I was thinking..." Saoirse paused, tapping an index finger to her lips. "Since you're open to wearing an elf costume part of the year, what about a leprechaun costume?"

Donner worked as the Head Elf at the Yule Heights Shopping Mall annual mall Santa meet and greet. He was a bit grumpy and definitely not super great with kids, but somehow, they loved him and he was almost more of a hit than Santa was. They flocked to him just because he wanted nothing to do with them, or at least that's how it seemed. In the bar, however, he took more of a behind-the-scenes approach, which she was fine with because he was so dependable.

Donner shot her daggers with the expression in his eyes. "Elves are happy, helpful creatures. They don't associate with leprechauns."

She lifted one brow, an amused smile spilling onto her lips. "And *you* identify as happy and helpful?"

"I'm a gosh dang delight," he reminded her, his face still stoic and unmoving—a complete mismatch from the words coming out of his mouth. "Ho ho ho."

With that, he turned around and headed back into the kitchen, letting the door swing behind him.

"Wrong holiday!" she called after him.

St. Patrick's Day was right around the corner, and it had been a scramble to get through closing on the bar and setting up the business license in time to open on such a specific day. It was incredibly important that they didn't miss this holiday, though, given the theme of the entire bar and its name. Thankfully, the establishment that she had purchased was already a fully operating bar at the time, so aside from changing out the hideous and old decor, redoing the branding, and restocking the inventory she wanted, it hadn't been a huge amount of work to reopen.

Technically, they were open now and had stayed open throughout the transition. She glanced around the main room; a few customers sitting at the high top tables watching a game on the television mounted on the wall. She assumed they were probably regulars of the establishment before she bought it since she hadn't done any major marketing yet about opening. But the push for the grand opening party on St. Patrick's Day was well underway on social media and she had invited every Instagram influencer over twenty-one years old in a thirty-mile radius.

The front door to the bar opened with a creaking sound, and Saoirse glanced up from the notebook she was writing in. A tall woman with thick, dark purple streaks in her midnight-black hair walked in, paused, and looked around the room.

As a new owner, Saoirse wanted to ask her what she thought about the changes, but she also couldn't help and notice what the woman was wearing. Her smooth, brown skin shone against the white collared shirt she had on—it was definitely a man's work shirt with a French tuck in the front into a pair of cropped black pants. Bright purple suspenders traveled up her torso from the waistband of her pants and disappeared behind her shoulders, accentuating her shape even in the slightly bulky shirt she was wearing. A few inches of lower legs showed off before black, high-heeled ankle boots ended the entire look.

The woman's gaze met hers and Saoirse felt her face flame with heat, looking back down at her notebook. How long had she been staring? *My gosh, how embarrassing.* It wasn't like she was desperate or anything, but it had been over a year since she'd ended her last engagement a few days before the planned wedding, and she hadn't dated anyone in the time since. She'd been so focused on building a new life, starting fresh, that there really hadn't been time to date even if she'd wanted to.

Not to mention she hadn't left her ex on the best of terms, and that was probably still a conversation she needed to have one day.

"Are you the new owner?" A voice interrupted her thoughts as someone pulled out bar stool and sat down in front of her.

She looked up to see the woman she'd been staring at seconds ago. "Yes. I'm Saoirse. Nice to meet you, and thanks for coming in."

"I've been coming here a long time, so I'm interested to see what you do with the place," the woman admitted, taking in the changes as she looked around. She seemed pleased with it...or at the very least, not horrified. "I'm Nell, by the way."

"Can I get you something to drink, Nell?" she asked, putting her pen down on top of the notebook. It rolled off the edge and hit the wooden bar top with a clatter. "Wine? Beer?"

"Whiskey ginger, neat." Nell placed her cell phone down on the bar top and propped herself up on her elbows.

Saoirse nodded and quickly went about prepping the drink, completely mindful of the fact that Nell was watching her intensely the entire time. She placed the full glass down in front of her on top of a cocktail napkin. "Anything else? Are you hungry? The kitchen is almost open, so we can get something started for you."

Nell shook her head. "I'm fine with this for now." She took a sip of the drink, and her eyes closed briefly, as if she was savoring it.

Saoirse wasn't sure what she was feeling, but something about this woman being so close made her nervous—in a good way. She wanted to impress her or strike up a conversation about something...anything.

So why was her mind drawing a complete blank on the ability to speak right now?

"It's great to see a woman owning this place finally," Nell interrupted her anxious thoughts. "I loved TJ's, but it's about time more women owned businesses in this mall. My best friend opened the arcade on the other side a few years back, and she could use the company."

Saoirse glanced toward the entrance, which spilled out into the Yule Heights Shopping Mall main corridor. There was another entrance on the opposite side of the bar that went directly to the street, but from what she could tell so far, the majority of customers tended to trickle in after shopping, or at the end of a work shift.

"I've walked past that arcade. It looks fun," she admitted. "Maybe you can ask her to come to the launch on the seventeenth with you? I'd love to get to know the other store owners."

"Who says I'm coming to the launch?" Nell smirked

slightly, her head tilting to the side with a mischievous look. "Or is that an invitation?"

Saoirse quickly tried to look anywhere but at Nell directly. "Uh, I mean, yeah. Everyone is invited. The more, the merrier, right?"

Nell nodded, but the smirk stayed put. "I'll tell Mara to come. She's going to want a green beer though."

Finally, a topic she could talk on without sounding foolish. "We will definitely have that. Themed cocktails, too. Though, I'm still coming up with those."

"Need any help?" Nell offered as she sipped her drink again. She pushed a lock of purple hair behind her ear. "I have an eye for that kind of thing."

"Really?" Saoirse raised her brows. "What do you suggest?"

She looked off into the distance for a moment, her expression seeming deep in thought. When she turned to look back at Saoirse, there was a smile on her face. "Can I come back there?"

Saoirse cleared her throat, then nodded. "Uh, yeah. Sure."

Nell looked like a kid in a candy store as she walked behind the bar and started pulling out different bottles. "Where do you keep the limes?"

She handed her a container full of pre-sliced limes. "What are you making?"

"I call it the Irish Kiss," Nell revealed as she put the finishing touches on a green-tinted drink on ice. She squeezed the lime slice into it and tossed it in the drink, then stirred it with a small straw. "Here, try it."

Saoirse took the glass from her and sipped through the straw. It was sweet and sour all at the same time and packed a punch with the whiskey hidden inside. "Oh, wow. That's actually really good. Can I use this for the launch?"

Nell seemed proud of herself. "Sure. I have a few other ideas, if you want."

She absolutely wanted all the help she could get, and whoever Nell was, she definitely had a knack for mixing flavors. Saoirse nodded vigorously and was about to say yes before a man called her attention from the front entrance.

"Hey, are you Saoirse Walsh?" he asked as he walked up to the bar. Slightly below average height, the man was wearing a puffy parka and jeans. His sneakers looked like they hadn't been washed once since he'd purchased them, and when he reached the bar, he placed a recorder down on the bar top. "I'm Dick from Yule Heights Times. I was hoping to interview you about the opening."

She plastered on her best smile for the man, but immediately felt a churning in her gut. Something about his presence told her that he had zero interest in helping her market the launch, and all the interest in exploiting her past.

"Sure, Dick. Happy to chat," she lied. "What questions do you have?"

"Do any of your exes own part of the bar, or are you the full owner?" he asked. "Three, right?"

Saoirse frowned. "Why would they own part of the bar? I own it alone. I bought it."

"Makes sense," Dick replied. "Since you never officially got married. What do you think keeps holding you back?"

"Excuse me?" *What the hell.*

"What's your issue with walking down the aisle?" Dick repeated, somehow oblivious to how annoyed she was at his line of questioning. "It's fascinating, you know? Readers are going to want to know what made you walk away three times—or is it better to say run away?" He laughed at his joke, then looked at her expectantly. "I can't imagine living out the plot of a movie in real life. Tell me, do you think Julia Roberts would ever agree to endorse The Lucky Leprechaun?"

Saoirse licked her lips, trying to bite back the response she wanted to give. As if she hadn't heard the joke comparing her to The Runaway Bride film more than a few dozen times. "I'm not sure how this is relevant to your article."

"Well, it's a humanities piece," Dick tried to explain, as if she actually wanted to know. *How oblivious was this man?* "What makes someone end three engagements and move to another state and open a bar? Are you afraid of marriage, or do you just love being single?"

"I think you've got your information wrong, Dick," Nell suddenly jumped into the conversation as she placed a bright green cocktail down on the bar in front of him.

Saoirse had completely forgotten she was standing there behind the bar, but the look on Nell's face was pure fire.

And she wasn't done. "Saoirse isn't single, and she isn't afraid of marriage. She and I are married. She moved here to be with me."

"Really?" Dick's brows lifted so high they almost ran into his hairline. He looked between them for verification.

"Uh." She cleared her throat. That was certainly not the response she'd expected. "Yes, well...um, it's a long story."

"So, you're finally married?" Dick pulled out a notepad from his back pants pocket and started scrawling with a pen he found in his jacket pocket. "Fourth time is the charm, huh?"

Nell narrowed her eyes into small slits. "Dick, can I get your business card? I'd love to chat with your editor."

He seemed to get the hint at her tone. "Uh, well, you

know, it's probably out in my car. I think I've got enough information now, anyway. Thanks."

With that, he turned and skittered away, leaving the bar quickly. Saoirse watched him for a moment and then looked at Nell.

She put her hands up, questioning. "Nell, what the heck was that? *We're married?*"

CHAPTER THREE

NELL

NELL DID NOT HAVE a prepared response for Saoirse's baffled exclamation. After all, this entire plan was based on a passive aggressive whim toward a nosy man and not thought through for more than a split second. That alone was strange enough for her to wonder where it had come from. Her entire career and life were centered around ignoring men who underestimated her or made judgments about her. Normally, she'd have not even paid attention to Dick's line of questions and just enjoyed her drink.

But something about the way Saoirse had tensed up with each additional question—her body literally curling in on itself in an attempt to get away from him and his intrigue. She couldn't stand down in that moment. Nell felt protective and defensive, and then the entire fake marriage story just blurted out of her before she was even able to realize what she was saying.

"Uh, well..." She walked from behind the bar and took a seat in front of Saoirse. It had felt weird still being back there after she'd just plowed through an emotional boundary of relationship status as well as physical boundaries of bar space. "He was being *so* judgmental. I just wanted to get rid of him, and that shut him up. It's the only thing I could think of in the moment."

Saoirse leaned forward on the bar, her brows knitting together. "What if he publishes that we're married, though? How exactly does that shut him up?"

Nell blinked. "Uh, well...I hadn't thought that far ahead. It was more of an impulse decision."

"Impulse marriages are for Vegas," Saoirse said, now crossing her arms over her chest, her nostrils flaring. "We're in Michigan, Nell."

She laughed a bit at that statement, but the hardened stare on Saoirse's face made it catch in her throat. She coughed instead.

"We could tell him we got divorced?" Nell offered, cringing as she leaned back on the stool.

Saoirse huffed, and her eyes rolled so hard that even Nell could feel it. "So, I left three people at the altar and divorced the fourth? That is *not* a better story, Nell. I don't even know your last name!"

Fair point. "Okay, so obviously it's not a great explanation, but I bet it's enough to get him off your tracks until after the grand opening," Nell argued. "They're only doing this humanities piece because of the turnover in ownership, right? So, in a month or two, things die down and he won't even check back in to see if we're still married or not."

"We're not married," Saoirse repeated emphatically. "But you're right. With a little time, it'll probably blow over. I doubt the Yule Heights Times is that much of a stickler for details and fact-checking."

Nell wasn't so sure about that, but she kept her mouth shut. No need to stir the flames of the fire she'd set.

"Okay, this could work." Saoirse was pacing back and

forth behind the bar now, and Nell wasn't about to interrupt her line of thinking. "We'd have to get on the same page. Learn some facts about each other. At least enough to throw him off next time he comes around for more answers."

"Or if he publishes that, then people around town are probably going to ask," Nell added. "It would be good to have our story straight."

"Starting with, what's your full name?" Saoirse pulled out two small shot glasses from behind the bar and then grabbed a bottle of whiskey. She quickly filled both up and pushed one toward Nell.

"Nell James. And you're Saoirse Walsh." She took the shot glass and sniffed the liquor. She could already feel it burning in her stomach and she hadn't even taken a sip yet. "Are we turning this into a drinking game?"

"I have to be a little drunk to try to make this make sense in my head," Saoirse confirmed. "Otherwise, I'd probably just call security and have you kicked out."

Nell laughed and shook her head. "Okay, fair enough, but I've been coming here for years. Don't take away my home away from home. They know me here."

Something on Saoirse's face softened at that response. "That's my goal for this place—to give people a home away from home. Some sort of safe harbor to recharge alone or with friends, you know?"

Nell didn't respond immediately, wondering if home was something Saoirse had had much of before.

"Is Nebraska home to you?" Nell asked, recalling some details from the article she'd read.

Saoirse shook her head emphatically. "I burned that bridge. Left complete carnage in my wake, actually." She laughed lightly, but it was hollow and something about the sound made Nell's chest hurt. "Imagine being one of the only two people in a hundred-mile radius who is open about their sexuality—and then breaking up with that person."

Nell was only slightly familiar with that feeling, but thankfully Yule Heights wasn't as isolated as it sounded like Saoirse's hometown had been. They were about an hour from Detroit, but with a little leg work, it was possible to find communities around here that felt welcoming of her sexual orientation. "I'm sorry," she said. "That sounds rough."

"Drink up." Saoirse lifted the glass to her lips and took the entire shot in one go.

Nell followed suit, but she needed a few swallows to get it all down, and even then she coughed and choked on the fiery liquid. "Christ. That burns."

Saoirse grinned, and an ease took over her expression that Nell hadn't seen yet. "Okay, your turn. Tell me something about you."

She thought for a moment, placing the shot glass down on the bar top. Saoirse filled it back up, along with hers. "I have a pet snake."

Her eyes widened. "What?"

"Yeah, Laura Dern. She's a Rosy Boa, and about two and a half feet in length." Nell stretched out her arms to the approximate length she guessed. "I've had her about five years now."

"You named your snake Laura Dern?" Saoirse was smiling again, and Nell couldn't help but notice the bright green flecks sparkle in her hazel eyes. "Like from The Ellen Show episode in the 90s?"

She both was and wasn't surprised that Saoirse immediately knew the reference. She tapped the tip of her nose with her pointer finger. "Ding, ding, ding!"

"I don't know how I feel about living with a snake," Saoirse joked. "What if that's a marriage dealbreaker?"

"Hey, Laura Dern was here first," Nell teased, tossing back more easily the second shot of whiskey that Saoirse had poured them both. "You'll have to learn to love her. We're a package deal."

"Plus, we're already married, so not much I can do about it now," Saoirse teased.

Nell could tell the liquor was settling into Saoirse's stomach now with the way her voice had changed. Nothing major, but she just sounded looser...calmer. The tension that had been there when Dick had been asking his questions had eased and they felt like...friends.

"Okay, my turn," Saoirse said, clearing her throat. "I have two tattoos."

She scanned the bare parts of Saoirse's body that she could see—her arms, neck, and a slight gap between the hem of her shirt and the top of her jeans—but she didn't see any ink. "Really? Where?"

A smirk crossed Saoirse's lips before she straightened it. "One on my thigh—a four leaf clover as an homage to my Irish roots. Another on my ribs—the serenity prayer."

"On your ribs?" Nell lifted her brows. "That's a really painful spot to get ink—right on the bone."

"Freaking brutal." Saoirse nodded and grabbed the hem of her shirt, hiking it up to show the skin on her side, which —aside from the dark ink—was so light that it was almost blinding in the dimly lit bar. It was a minimalist font, barely legible but beautifully delicate.

Nell leaned a little closer to read the words of the prayer. "Does that prayer have special meaning to you?"

She nodded. "My...well, not to trauma dump, but my father was an alcoholic and I never really knew him aside from the few times he'd show up drunk and ask my mother for money. When I was in college, my mother died—ovarian cancer. She had never moved on after him—still loved him—and he didn't even come to her funeral. I got a collect call from him once last year, but other than that, no idea where he is. And I don't really care."

Nell's eyes traveled past Saoirse to the wall of liquor bottles behind her. It was an interesting choice of careers after a family history like that, and something about the daring and rebellious nature of it made Nell like her even more. "I'm sorry that happened," she said. "I grew up in the foster system, so absent parents are sort of my area of expertise."

"Really?" Saoirse seemed surprised by that admission, then pointed to the work badge hanging on a lanyard around Nell's neck from earlier that she'd forgotten to remove. "And now you're a fancy scientist? That's quite the glow up."

She fingered the badge, and then slid it over her head and tucked it into her bag. "Yeah, I love what I do. I was lucky. When I was a teenager, I was finally adopted by a really nice couple in town along with another kid in the foster program with me. I kept my last name as homage to my roots, but they changed my life. Dash is like a brother to me now. In fact, he and his wife just had their second child, so I'm an aunt again, too."

Saoirse smiled widely at that. "A little jealous about that, to be honest. Kids are fun."

"So are snakes," Nell joked.

"Less sure about that one." Saoirse shook her head, but then lined up two more shot glasses and poured them another round. "Okay, next question. When was your last date?"

Nell could feel her cheeks heat at the memory that was flashing before her eyes. "Uh, well...it's not exactly recent."

Saoirse lifted one brow, a smirk on her lips. "No judgement here—I'm the runaway bride, remember?"

Nell grinned as she nodded. "It was about a year ago... actually, it was last Valentine's Day. So, I guess more than a year now."

"That's not that long. Who was the lucky lady?" Saoirse asked.

"This is where you're going to judge me." Nell had not told this story to anyone, and it was boggling her mind that she had already shared this much. "It was my landlord's ex-wife."

Saoirse's eyes almost bugged out of her face. "Does your landlord know?"

Nell shook her head adamantly, because that was the absolute last thing that she needed. She loved her townhouse and wasn't ready to move anytime soon. In fact, she was hoping the landlord would want to sell the entire place, and she could buy it off him.

"Holy cow, that's awkward." Saoirse laughed. "I guess you have a thing for wives, or almost-wives."

"It does seem to be a pattern," Nell admitted with a chuckle, even though that was the only experience she'd had with someone who'd once been married. "Everyone has some sort of past. I try to never hold that against who someone is today."

Saoirse poured another shot, and Nell glanced at it as she felt her stomach sloshing. "Should we do one more?"

"Why not?" Nell shrugged, though the little voice in the back of her mind said *don't do it.*

Saoirse lifted her brows. "Are you sure? I'm a bartender, so I can go quite a few rounds. How's a scientist's tolerance?"

That sealed the deal for Nell—a challenge. She pulled the now-filled shot glass toward her and tapped the bottom against the wooden bar top. "I can take it. I'm a regular here, you know."

"Yeah, but you strike me as a one, maybe two, drink regular before you're home watching Netflix in wool socks and a throw blanket."

Nell grinned, because that was a more than slightly accurate representation of her nights off. "Bottoms up," she said, lifting the glass to her lips and tipping her head back.

Her throat opened and she took a long swallow, and that was the last thing she remembered until she woke up the next morning.

CHAPTER FOUR

SAOIRSE

Why are exposed pipes on my bedroom ceiling? Saoirse frowned as she blinked slowly back to consciousness and stared up. Her head felt heavy, but she managed to shift it an inch to the right and glance around the room.

Maybe because this isn't my bedroom. She took in her worn office furniture and the Federal Labor Law posters on the wall. Had she spent the night in the back office at the bar?

She slid her tongue across her bottom lip, chapped and dry. Clearing her throat, she stretched out her legs, but was immediately met with resistance. When she lifted her head to look down at her feet, the room took a few spins before being right-side up, but she finally focused her vision and realized that she had four feet now.

How much did I freaking drink? Saoirse pushed to sit up, but something pulled her back to the couch, and she quickly realized it was an arm. But, not *her* arm. Saoirse stretched her neck to look behind her on the couch and saw Nell asleep with one arm around her waist and her legs intertwined with hers.

The memories from last night came back quickly. She was married—sort of. Nell was a customer from the bar—a beautiful one. And they'd gone shot for shot until the bar closed. Had they kissed? Had they done *more* than kiss? Saoirse took inventory of her clothes, but everything seemed to be on in the right order, no indication that she'd taken anything off.

Maybe they'd just passed out like this together because they'd both been too tired? That didn't explain the spooning, though. Or why she didn't feel alarmed by the entire experience in the least. Instead, she rotated her body slowly and carefully so that she was lying on the couch facing the still-sleeping Nell instead of butt to crotch like they'd been a moment ago.

Nell was incredibly beautiful. She'd thought so last night, but having an unfiltered moment to just look at the russet-toned, purple-haired woman as she slept only confirmed it for her. Her hair was somewhere in between short and long—possibly just long enough to touch her shoulders, but it was hard to tell from them both being horizontal. Black roots were beginning to show at the crown of her hair where the purple highlights needed touch ups, but Saoirse loved that little bit of realism in the moment.

Her own hair was dark red and stringy with a bit of a straw texture to it that she'd been trying to combat with different deep conditioners over the years. Funny, since everyone she met spoke about how much they loved her hair, but she was the first person to critique it in the mirror every morning. Nell didn't seem the type to do that, and she bet that she loved her body as it was.

"What are you thinking?" Nell's lips moved and Saoirse was caught off guard.

"Oh! I thought you were sleeping," she admitted.

Nell's eyes fluttered open, clearly heavy with sleep still. "I was." She yawned and stretched her body. "But then you turned around."

Saoirse smiled. "Sorry to wake you."

"Don't be. You seemed deep in thought," Nell repeated.

"I was thinking about how much I love your hair," she admitted. "I tend to be pretty insecure about mine, so I was comparing myself."

"That's never a good idea," Nell replied with a chuckle. "Comparison is the thief of joy. Plus, I love your hair." Nell reached forward and slid her fingers through Saoirse's hair in a gentle caress. She lingered at the ends, then allowed her hand to fall to Saoirse's waist instead. "It's beautiful."

She could feel her cheeks heating, and her core tightened at Nell's compliment. She wanted to lean forward and kiss her right then, but that seemed too much, too soon. She wasn't sure. What *had* they done last night?

Aside from getting fake-married.

"I should probably get up before the Saturday employees come in and see us here," Saoirse admitted, though even she could hear the hesitation in her own voice. She pushed up off the couch, untangling her legs from Nell as she rose.

Nell nodded, lifting herself into a seated position on the couch. "I actually need to get home and feed Laura Dern."

It took Saoirse a moment to remember that Nell had named her snake that. "Can I meet her?"

The young woman seemed surprised. "You want to meet my snake?"

"When you say it like that, it sounds weird." Saoirse laughed, because admittedly that was a strange thing to ask someone. She wasn't even sure where it had come from, since she didn't like snakes. *I mean, does anyone like snakes?*

Nell, apparently.

"It *is* weird," Nell replied, now joining her on her feet. She grabbed her sweater off the back of the couch and pulled it on. "But, sure. I'm pretty hungry anyway. Want to do breakfast at my place?"

Saoirse's stomach growled in response. "Actually, that would be amazing. I could definitely eat."

Nell smirked at that comment, then gestured towards the door. "I'll drive us. Hopefully, my car is still in the lot."

A few minutes later, they were pulling into a small neighborhood of matching townhomes secluded from the main roads. Saoirse admired the manicured lawns and spirited St. Patty's Day decorations on the homes as they drove by. Her own apartment was in an older building in town that was more than a few years past due for some remodels.

"This place is gorgeous," Saoirse complimented Nell as they pulled into a short driveway in front of an end-unit townhouse—all brick with thick bushes in front of the exterior and black trim around the doors and windows. "How long have you lived here?"

"A few years now. I'm hoping to buy it off the landlord when he's ready to sell," Nell said, as she opened the car door and stepped out.

Saoirse followed suit and walked behind her up to the front door, pausing as Nell unlocked it and ushered them both in.

"Meet Laura Dern." Nell gestured toward a large glass terrarium tank on the far end of the living room.

They walked closer and Saoirse scanned the length of the tank but didn't see the snake. "What does she look like? I think she's blending in."

Nell stopped in front of the tank and peered inside. She

frowned, then pushed up on her toes to look over the top of the tank. "Uh oh. The lid is askew."

"What?" Nell felt her skin prickling into goosebumps. "The lid is open?"

"Yup." Nell stepped back and looked around the living room. "Well, she's around here somewhere. We'll find her."

"THE SNAKE IS LOOSE?" Saoirse immediately grabbed Nell's arm and hid behind her, as if Nell was some sort of snake shield that would protect her from...what?

"She's very friendly," Nell assured her with a laugh, but didn't try to push her off her arm. Instead, Nell placed a hand over hers. "Let's look for her together. Okay?"

Saoirse nodded, but her voice felt like it was stuck in her throat.

Then Nell's cell phone rang, interrupting their search-and-rescue plans.

"Hello?" Nell answered it, then whispered to Saoirse that it would just be one second. "Hey, Mara. What's up?"

She was quiet for a moment, listening to the woman on the other end. Saoirse couldn't stop scanning the room, looking for any movement or slithering. It was one thing to see a snake named after a gay icon behind glass, but having it run up her leg or tickle her feet was not an option Saoirse could get behind.

"He called you?" Nell's eyes widened, and Saoirse's attention was pulled back to the phone call.

She frowned and whispered, "Who?"

"Dick," Nell whispered back, her hand over the speaker. "The reporter is calling my friends to fact-check us."

She grimaced. "What did she say?"

Nell put one finger up as she returned to the call and thanked her friend. She hung up the phone and slid it into her pocket. "Well, thankfully Mara just said no comment."

Saoirse lifted her brows. "Really? That was nice of her."

"Yeah, but then she called me immediately because she thinks I didn't invite her to my wedding." Nell laughed and shook her head. "If I didn't let her be my maid of honor, I'm pretty sure she'd murder me in my sleep."

She felt a surge of jealousy roll through her core at the way Nell was speaking about this other woman. Surely they were just friends, but the image of Nell being close to another woman made her tense up and she didn't even know why. It wasn't like they were dating, or even together. Were they? Is this what the beginning of dating looked like? Was Nell even interested in her in that way?

Saoirse swallowed hard, because even if Nell did want to open that door, she couldn't let her. Not with her reputation. Nell seemed like a good person, and clearly she had a bright future in her career. Saoirse wasn't about to saddle her with the runaway bride bartender back story after all Nell had done to bring herself out the foster care system and into a successful career in science.

"Oh, I think I know where she is!" Nell put a hand up, then gestured for Saoirse to follow her.

They went up a flight of stairs and down a short hallway before walking into a room with a large king-sized bed in it. The entire room looked like a bachelor pad—brown, black, and leather everything. In fact, the only spot of color in the entire room was a thick, shaggy, bright green throw blanket tossed over one corner of the bed.

"Is this your bedroom?" Saoirse asked. She walked over to a large painting on the wall that was multiple shades of dark blue and featured a woman from the back as she curled into herself. It was beautifully painted, but it felt heavy and sad.

"Yeah, and Laura Dern is always hiding in my bed."

Nell pulled back the dark brown comforter and scanned the sheets. "Well, she usually is."

Saoirse sat on the black leather bench at the end of her bed and leaned forward, her elbows on her knees. "You have very specific taste," she joked, still scanning the room. "Do you collect those?"

Nell glanced where she was pointing to a series of vases in different sizes and shapes in the corner or the room. "It's supposed to be fancy decor. I have no idea. A girl I dated bought them—she was into design and architecture and said my house was too eclectic. She was always trying to push me to make it more model-home like."

"Oh." Saoirse felt the tickle of jealousy again but pushed it down.

"She didn't succeed," Nell assured her, coming to sit next to her on the wide bench. "Wait till you see my kitchen —cocks everywhere."

"What?" She laughed, finding herself leaning a bit closer to Nell.

"Like chickens," Nell finished. She was laughing hard now, clearly knowing how she made that sound. "It's a rooster-themed kitchen."

"What a specific choice for a lesbian kitchen," Saoirse joked back.

Nell smiled but was quiet for a moment as her gaze lowered to Saoirse's lips, then returned to her eyes. Saoirse said nothing, but she could feel her chest tightening as it suddenly felt more difficult to breathe.

"Do you think we kissed last night?" Nell asked, her voice soft and throaty in a way that made Saoirse's skin shiver.

"I can't remember," she replied, her own voice sounding raspy. She slid her tongue across her bottom lip, wanting nothing more than to feel Nell pressed against her. "I wish I did."

And then Nell leaned in, and Saoirse's eyes closed in anticipation of her lips against hers. What she hadn't anticipated, however, was the scratchy, flickering feeling of something licking her ankle and then wrapping around it as it moved up her leg.

Saoirse's eyes popped open so fast as she bounced up off the bench, screaming at the top of her lungs. "IT'S TOUCHING ME!"

Nell looked startled, taking a second to figure out what was going on. She glanced down at Saoirse's feet and then smiled widely. "Oh, there's Ms. Dern!"

"GET IT OFF ME!" Saoirse shrieked as she froze in spot and closed her eyes. Maybe she could just disappear right here and she'd be able to rewind to before the time she ever touched a snake. "IT'S GOING TO BITE ME!"

"She doesn't bite," Nell assured her as she quickly stood and unwound the long snake from Saoirse's ankle. It wrapped around Nell's forearm and slid its tongue back out in a quick flicker toward Saoirse.

She, of course, jumped back eight feet, her hand to her chest. "I think I'm going to pass out."

Nell shook her head, but there was an amused smirk on her face. "Go lie down in the bed for a second. I'll put her away downstairs."

Saoirse eyed her cautiously as she walked past her, the snake still in her hands. After Nell left, she made her way shakily over to the bed and sat on the edge. It was softer than she expected it to be, and she ran her hand across the sheets imagining what it would be like to lie in this bed next to Nell.

She quickly tried to push the thought away from her

mind—why was she getting so ahead of herself? It wasn't like she even had time to date or pursue any romantic interest. She had a bar to open, and she was just days away from their grand opening and was petrified of Nell's scaly roommate.

"How about some breakfast?" Nell called up from downstairs. "I'll cook something and bring it up."

"Sure," Saoirse called back, feeling cared for in that moment.

When was the last time anyone had made her breakfast? She lay back against the mattress and sighed at herself.

What the hell am I doing?

CHAPTER FIVE

NELL

It had been a while since she'd had a woman in her bed, but when Nell walked back into her room to see Saoirse fast asleep on top of the covers, it didn't feel strange at all. It felt nice...comforting. It felt like they'd done this before, like they hadn't just met last night.

She placed the tray of eggs and toast on the bed next to her guest and gently rubbed her shoulder. "Sersh? You hungry?"

The ginger-haired woman roused from sleep and yawned. "Wow, that smells amazing."

Nell sat cross-legged on the bed next to her as Saoirse sat up and did the same. She handed her a fork and a plate, and they both started eating their breakfast as if they hadn't eaten in days. A few bites in, and she was already feeling a million times better after how she'd woken up that morning with a belly full of liquor and a brain full of foggy memories from the night before.

They didn't talk for a few moments, but Nell caught Saoirse glancing up at her. They exchanged shy smiles and returned to their food.

"I should probably get back to the bar soon. Well, I should go home and shower first, then get back to the bar." Saoirse had finished her plate of food and put it down. "The grand opening is almost here. I've got so much to do."

Nell frowned at the stressed expression on Saoirse's face as she finished her last few bites. "You can shower here. Looks like we wear the same size clothes, so you can just borrow something of mine. Unless you want to go home, of course."

She eyed her for a moment. "It would actually be a big time-saver to shower here instead of going across town and back again."

"Perks of living close to the bar," Nell replied, placing her empty plate down next to Saoirse's. "Why do you think I'm a regular there?"

Saoirse grinned and lifted one brow. "I thought it was for the company."

"The company is a big plus," Nell replied, picking up their plates and putting them on the nightstand before turning back to face Saoirse. "I think I'm pretty interested in the new ownership."

"Really?" Saoirse bit the edge of her lip in a way that made Nell's core heat. "I hear the new owner is a bit of a wild card."

Nell didn't respond to that, but instead leaned forward and placed her lips against Saoirse's. She seemed to freeze for a moment, as if holding her breath, but when Nell's hand lifted to the back of her neck, Saoirse melted forward.

She pressed into her, one hand cupping Nell's jaw and the other resting on her knee. Her tongue slid across her bottom lip, and Nell felt a different kind of hunger fill her. The moment dragged out in what felt like the longest, most perfect kiss of her life, and yet, when Saoirse pulled away, it still felt too soon.

"I—I should go." Saoirse's voice was raspy. She cleared her throat. "I have a lot to do for the opening."

Nell's gaze dropped to her lips, then returned to meet hers. She wanted to grab her and kiss her again, but the look of nervousness in Saoirse's eyes stopped her. "Okay."

Saoirse scrambled off the bed quickly, heading for the door of the bedroom. She paused in the door frame and glanced back at Nell. "You'll be there, right? At the opening?"

She smiled. "I wouldn't miss it."

The redhead nodded then headed down the hallway. Nell heard the front door of her house open and then close. She lay back on the mattress and let out a loud exhale. Had that just happened? She felt like sometimes her life had become so routine that there wasn't space for someone else in it, or she wouldn't even know how to welcome someone in.

But something about Saoirse fit into her life like she'd always been meant to be there.

Nell's thoughts were interrupted by the doorbell. She frowned and got up, heading downstairs. When she opened her front door, Saoirse was standing on the front steps looking even more awkward than before and fidgeting with her hands.

"Uh, I just remembered that you drove us here," Saoirse said, pointing toward Nell's car in the driveway. "I might need a ride back. Or can I borrow your phone to call a Lyft?"

Nell laughed and grabbed her car keys out of the bowl on the small table by the front door. "I completely forgot, too. I'll drive us back."

"Can I actually take that shower really quickly first?" Saoirse asked, a bashful smile on her face.

"Christ," Nell said, stepping aside and ushering her in. "Seems we forgot about everything."

"I think we had a good reason," Saoirse joked. "Towel?"

Nell escorted her back upstairs and grabbed her a towel from the linen closet and then showed her how to adjust the hot and cold water in the shower, since it was pretty finicky. She left her alone in the bathroom and closed the door behind her, then headed downstairs to distract herself. She couldn't just stand there and think about Saoirse naked on the other side of that door with water running across her smooth skin.

Instead, she busied herself with feeding Laura Dern, watering her plants on the windowsill, and washing the breakfast dishes in the kitchen sink. By the time she was done, Saoirse was walking down the stairs in a plain white T-shirt and light-wash skinny jeans that Nell recognized as being hers.

"I hope you don't mind, but I grabbed some clothes from your drawers. I can wash and return them." She looked nervous. "I just didn't want to show up at work in the same clothes as yesterday."

"It's fine," Nell assured her. "You can return them next time you're here."

"So, I'm coming back?" Saoirse offered a flirty smile as Nell grabbed her car keys and opened the front door.

"I hope so." She reached a hand out to squeeze Saoirse's, but then intertwined their fingers and pulled her close. They kissed softly, quickly, before pulling apart again. "Come on. Let's get you back to work."

"I mean, I can be late..." Saoirse kidded as she followed her to the car.

Nell was darn close to being tempted, but she knew how important this opening was to Saoirse. She wasn't going to be the one to distract the bar owner from doing everything she needed to do to make it a success. When she dropped her off at the mall a few minutes later, they said goodbye and Nell promised to come to the grand opening later that night.

Still feeling pretty tired, Nell stopped at the local Starbucks on the way back home. She ordered a triple shot espresso and waited by the counter until they called her name.

"Nell James?" A different voice called from behind her as she picked up her coffee.

She turned to see Professor Abby Moore sitting at one of the tables in the lobby, a sugary Frappuccino in front of her.

"Abby, or...uh, Professor Moore," Nell greeted the woman warmly and walked over to her table. They hadn't talked about how they'd address one another if they ran into each other in the future, so she didn't know what to say. She hadn't seen Professor Moore since she'd taken her graduate course and...other things. "Still drinking only Fraps, I see."

The slightly older woman smiled and held up the drink. "Sugar is still my weakness. It really gets me going."

Nell sat down in the chair across from her and smiled with a slight seductive lilt to her voice as she teased. "I seem to remember a few other things that get you going."

Abby's cheeks darkened, turning red as she looked down at the drink in her hands and fidgeted with the straw. "Fond memories."

Their love affair had been brief, and after she'd already taken and passed Abby's class. It had been Nell's first serious relationship with a woman. They'd spent just under a year together before Nell had graduated and moved back here.

"What are you doing in Yule Heights?" Nell asked, certainly not expecting to have seen her first girlfriend here today. "Are you still teaching at U of M?"

She nodded, immediately familiar with the reference to the school. "I am, but I have a friend who moved here. I just came to visit her."

"A friend?" Nell lifted one brow, sensing there was more to the story.

"Okay, an ex." Abby grinned, and Nell remembered how much she'd loved Abby's shyness. She was five years older than Nell, but Nell had always been the more dominant personality in their relationship. She'd appreciated that experience, as it had really helped her learn who she was and about who she wanted to be in a relationship going forward.

That being said, she and Abby had definitely not been a forever-fit for a lot more reasons than just location, and Nell couldn't help but think of Saoirse in that moment. The ease she felt around Saoirse was already miles ahead of how she'd felt around Abby after months of dating.

Strange how that could happen.

"A different ex?" Nell pried a bit further.

Abby nodded. "Small world, apparently."

"Apparently so," Nell agreed. She smiled at Abby and shook her head. "Crazy seeing you here, but it's nice to run into you again."

"Yeah, you too," Abby agreed. "We should catch up sometime."

"I'd like that," Nell agreed, though she didn't have any interest in setting up plans right now. Instead, she got up from the table and gave Abby a small wave. "I'll see you around."

Abby waved back, and Nell left Starbucks and climbed into her car with a renewed excitement to see Saoirse tonight. Running into her ex in the same town on the same day was a weird coincidence, but Nell was deciding to take it as a sign. Reflecting on who she'd been in graduate school, she realized that she truly was ready for a relationship now. Her career was going well, and her life was comfortable and happy. She loved being an aunt and a good friend, and she loved her home and her snake. But...she would really love to add the right woman to her life, and Saoirse felt like she might be just that.

CHAPTER SIX

SAOIRSE

"WHAT IF NO ONE COMES?" Saoirse turned to look at Donner after she scanned the fully decorated bar. It was like a leprechaun had thrown up in this place—green and cloverleafs everywhere. There was a photo booth area in the corner with funny props, and each table had an assortment of themed hats or headbands for people to wear. The menu was set—and also very green—and the kitchen was already prepping for the evening shift with every possible greasy pub food she could think of.

"It's a bar. That serves alcohol. On St. Patrick's Day." Donner rolled his eyes at her so hard she practically felt it. "We're going to be packed. Don't worry."

"I know, I know." She appreciated Donner's blunt affect, and the way he gave no shits about softening his approach. "I'm just nervous. It's a big day!"

"Okay." Donner's response was lackluster at best, and he walked to the back of the restaurant to finish replenishing all the tables with napkins and biodegradable green straws.

The front door to the restaurant swung open, the bell overhead tinkling to announce a new patron. Saoirse perked up, but then froze when she saw who was walking through the front door.

"Abby?"

The brunette's eyes found her, and she smiled before making her way across the bar to her. "Saoirse."

"You're...you're here." Saoirse let out a long breath. This was unexpected, to say the least. "I...uh...I didn't know you were coming."

What the heck is happening right now?

"I know," Abby replied, sliding into a seat at the bar and crossing one leg over her other knee. "But I think we should talk. I haven't seen you since you left me at the altar, you know."

Saoirse felt her face heating up. "It wasn't *at* the altar."

Abby shrugged. "Well, two days before our wedding is pretty much the same thing."

"Uh, okay," Saoirse fumbled to find her words. "Well, I'm kind of in the middle of something right now. The bar opens tonight, and we're expecting a lot of people. Hopefully, that is."

"Seems to be empty right now." Abby gestured toward the bar which *was* empty of customers and only had a few employees still setting things up. But technically they were open now, so she hoped people would come in soon. "Can we just talk for a moment?"

Saoirse nodded and tried to swallow the nerves in her stomach. She pulled out the chair next to Abby and perched herself on the edge. "Sure. Let's talk."

She could feel Abby's eyes boring into her but couldn't meet her gaze. When she'd first met Abby, she was months out of her second engagement to a man she'd met at a previous job. She'd never even been with a woman before, and everything about Abby had been new and unexpected, but beyond exciting. They'd met online, and their flirtation had only been virtual at first. In fact, the entire first year they were together, they hadn't met in person.

But then Saoirse had traveled to where Abby lived in Ann Arbor, and at the end of her trip, Abby had asked her to marry her. Saoirse had been caught up in the romance of the moment, because the last thing she'd wanted was to go back home and leave Abby...so she'd said yes.

She'd had to go back home eventually, however. And when she did, their relationship became strained. The distance was hard on them, and while they'd both traveled back and forth a few times to see each other, Saoirse began to feel her usual anxiety toward commitment when each trip seemed to be longer and longer. Abby had a job at the university there, so she couldn't move, and Saoirse was beyond mobile.

It was on her last drive up to see Abby that she'd stopped in Yule Heights on the way and fallen in love with this bar. It was the first time she'd realized that she wanted to do something for herself. She had spent all of her twenties at the whim of a romantic partner, doing what they wanted and needed to make their dreams work.

But she didn't have any of her own.

"You moved to Michigan." Hurt shimmered in Abby's eyes, and Saoirse felt a churning in her gut. "You moved here...but not with me. What happened, Saoirse?"

"I explained what I could in my email," Saoirse said, feeling like a jerk for even stooping to that level. Communication wasn't her strong suit and she was working on that. "I know I should have talked to you in person, but I...I was really struggling."

"I would have supported you finding your own identity, following your own dreams," Abby countered. "You didn't even give me the chance. You didn't even tell me that that was what you wanted."

Saoirse dropped her chin to her chest and shook her head. *Gosh, that was so fucked up.* She'd spent six months in therapy after leaving Abby, and learning how to self-advocate and speak up for herself was something she was only just beginning to feel more capable of. "That was shitty of me, Abby. But it wasn't just about me wanting to follow my dreams. We just...there was something missing."

A lot of somethings, but she didn't say that out loud.

Abby's expression looked somehow more wounded now. "Like what?"

"Ms. Walsh?" A man's voice interrupted their conversation and Saoirse looked up to see Dick, the Yule Heights Times reporter, standing next to them. "Do you have a minute to assist with fact-checking some of the dates in my article before it goes live later today?"

He held out a tablet to her, a document pulled up on it with the title *Kiss the Runaway Bride, She's Irish!* The first line was even worse than the title as Saoirse scanned it: *Ever felt like getting your heart broken at the altar? Well, you might be next because guess who just moved to Yule Heights.*

Saoirse gave him a withering look. "Seriously? This is what you're writing about me?"

"What?" Dick looked cluelessly at her. "It's a pun. Don't worry, no one is actually going to kiss you. I included in the article that you're married now. The runaway bride, finally off limits!"

Saoirse's stomach lurched as she heard a gasp leave Abby.

"What does he mean you're married now?" Abby asked, pushing out of her chair and standing to face them both.

Dick looked at Abby, seeming to realize she was

standing there for the first time. "Oh, I know you! You're Number Three, right?"

"Excuse me?" Abby cut her eyes into slits as she glared at the reporter. "Number Three?"

"Like the third person she left right before the wedding?" Dick pointed to Saoirse. "I swear I saw your picture before. Is that not you?"

Abby's mouth fell open and she looked at Saoirse, as if daring her to explain.

"Uh, well...this is all..." Saoirse cleared her throat. "I can explain. But honestly...do I have to? I mean, this article is rude."

She shoved the tablet back toward Dick, and he grabbed it before it fell.

"I'm going to publish it either way," he warned her, a haughty expression overtaking his face. "I was just doing you a courtesy by letting you read it first."

"I don't want to read it, and I don't want you to publish it," Saoirse snapped back. Maybe it was the awkwardness of the moment, or maybe she'd just finally reached her limit with this guy, but she found herself unloading her frustration on him. "Please leave the bar, and do not come back."

He lifted his chin and huffed. "Fine. But I'm putting this in the article."

"Be my guest," she replied, gesturing toward the front door. "Please include the part where you minimize women to being nothing more than their relationship history and make no mention of the difficulty it takes to be a female business owner."

His expression faltered for a moment at that, but then he set his jaw and stormed toward the door. It opened before he got there, and someone held it for him.

"Thanks," he said gruffly before disappearing outside.

Nell stepped inside the bar, letting the door close behind her. She was wearing a dark green tank top that hugged her curves perfectly over tiny denim shorts, and she'd painted a shamrock on her shoulder, right by the end of her collarbone. Saoirse's memory flickered to showing Nell her clover tattoo and wondered if Nell had painted that on herself as some sort of romantic gesture.

She smiled at Saoirse the moment she saw her, but then her gaze dipped to Saoirse's left and Nell's face froze.

"Saoirse, I think you need to explain what that man was talking about," Abby continued, oblivious to who had just walked into the bar. Her arms crossed over her chest, she looked downright angry now. "You're married?"

"No, no..." Saoirse found the words getting stuck in her throat as Nell came closer.

"Abby?" Nell said as she walked up to them. "What are you doing here?"

"You know each other?" Saoirse asked, her eyes widening.

Abby let her hands drop to her sides and gave Nell a smile that looked like she was relieved to see her. "Hey, again. Twice in one day must be some kind of sign."

What the heck is happening right now? Is Abby flirting with Nell?

"Uh, yeah." Nell looked a bit uncomfortable. "Are you here for the opening?"

"No." Abby shook her head, then angled her body back to facing Saoirse. "This is my ex that I was telling you about."

Nell's mouth was now the one to fall open, and Saoirse was pretty sure that she could disappear completely right now if she just closed her eyes and pretended none of this was happening.

"Saoirse is your ex?"

Abby seemed confused. "You know Saoirse?"

I'd like to disappear right now, please.

They both looked at her now, as if it was her turn to provide the explanation. What explanation she was supposed to give? "Uh...well...how do you two know each other?"

That seemed the safer response—turn it back on them.

"Abby was my first girlfriend in graduate school." Nell crossed her arms over her chest, and Saoirse tried not to notice the way it made her breasts push together. "Actually, she was my professor for a semester first, but then we dated for almost a year before I graduated and moved back here."

Why me?

"Cool, cool, cool." Saoirse's speech tumbled out of her like she had no control over what she was saying. *Please get me out of here right now.* "That's so funny. What a small world."

"Please tell me that Nell is not who you're married to now," Abby interrupted. "Is she who that reporter was talking about?"

"Uh..." Saoirse suddenly couldn't remember how to form words at all. *Maybe this is all a dream?* "Um..."

"Saoirse, tell me you didn't leave me at the altar for my ex-girlfriend," Abby repeated, this time with further details that really did not paint the best picture.

"You two were engaged?" Nell pointed between the two of them, her eyes even wider than before. "Good freaking lord, this is messy."

"Uh..." *Please, Earth, swallow me whole right now. PLEASE.*

"Saoirse!" Donner called from the swinging door to the kitchen. "The fryer isn't working!"

Saved by the part-time elf.

"Oh, I have to go check on that. Busy day, you know. Very important to have a working fryer." She then broke into a sprint and ran back into the kitchen, leaving the two women standing there in the bar, jaws still agape.

"Sounded like you needed an out," Donner said, the door swinging shut behind them as he held up a basket of fries. "I made some French fries for you."

Tears stung at her eyes. "The fryer isn't broken?"

He shook his head and placed the basket on the counter next to her. "Nah. It's fine, but I want a raise."

"You got it." She laughed, nodding her head and popping a boiling hot fry into her mouth in an attempt to stop herself from crying.

Her romantic history was a mess. She already knew that. Hell, everyone knew that. But, she'd been working hard to start over, start fresh. She'd gone to therapy—still *was* going sometimes—and she'd built a business for herself here. She'd built the beginnings of *something* with Nell, and the last thing she'd prepared for was for her mistakes to come back to haunt her.

But maybe that was *exactly* what she should have expected.

CHAPTER SEVEN

NELL

"Abby, I had no idea you two had history," Nell found herself saying in the strangest turn of events she'd ever experienced. She was highly aware of the fact that they were in a very public place, and she wasn't about to have some sort of lover's triangle spat in front of neighbors and potential co-workers.

The last thing she needed was Mr. Staffi's tuna breath laughing in the break room on Monday about the spectacle he witnessed over the weekend.

But Abby was glaring at her now, and Nell immediately got flashbacks to her ex-girlfriend's hot temper—one of the many reasons Nell hadn't seen a future there. Not that it had ever been anything extreme, but she had always had a tendency to go from zero to sixty in a way that pacifist-by-nature Nell hadn't been comfortable with.

"That's *quite* the coincidence, Nell." Abby was tapping one foot against the ground, and she had one hand propped on her hip. "What is this? Some sort of revenge scheme against me? Are you trying to win me back or something? This is *not* how to do it."

Nell blinked once, twice...three times before she could find the words to respond. "This is definitely not some scheme. It's just a super odd coincidence. I promise."

Not to mention that she had zero interest in rekindling a romance with Abby. Their earlier talk in the coffee shop had been nostalgic at best, but she hadn't given it another thought in the hours since.

There was only one woman she couldn't stop thinking about.

"I don't believe in coincidences, and the likelihood of my ex-girlfriend pairing up with my ex-fiancée is a little too on the nose to ignore. I'm waiting right here until you both explain this to me." She turned to face the kitchen door that Saoirse had just disappeared through and raised her volume. "Saoirse!"

"Hey!" Nell put her hands up in alarm and tried to shush her. "You can't just scream at her in the middle of her own bar. It's her grand opening tonight."

Abby narrowed her eyes and let out a huff of hot air. "Fine, then I'm just going back there."

With that, she stomped off toward the kitchen and Nell quickly chased, intervening before she reached the door.

"Listen, we're both heated, right? This is clearly a lot to absorb." Nell put both hands up defensively in an attempt to calm the situation. "Why don't we both just leave and take some time to calm down? Then tomorrow we can discuss it rationally, like adults, after her opening is finished."

"Well..." Abby's brows were furrowed tight and she didn't seem convinced.

"Come on, Abs. Don't you think that would be the most productive response?" Nell tried to reason. "We can all talk as friends, and not in the heat of the emotion."

Abby faltered finally, her expression softening a touch as her brows relaxed. "I have to be back in Ann Arbor by Monday for classes."

"Perfect, so brunch tomorrow? All three of us?" Nell offered for them both, even though she was pretty sure she'd have to perform a circus act to get Saoirse to show up at that brunch. But whatever she needed to do to soothe this situation, she would.

"Fine." Abby shoved her hands in the back pockets of her jeans, turning away from the kitchen door. "But this whole thing is bullshit and I just want that on record."

"I'm right there with ya," Nell joked, ushering her toward the front door and walking out behind her. She walked Abby to her car with an awkward wave and then got into the driver's seat of her own car a few spots over.

Abby's car pulled out of the mall parking lot in front of her, turning down main street, while Nell just circled the block before turning right back into The Lucky Leprechaun's lot. She put the car back in park and scanned around, just to make sure Abby hadn't done the same thing.

The coast seemed clear, so she got out of her car and headed back into the bar—this time making a beeline right for the kitchen.

"Saoirse?" she called out when she entered, but Donner was the only one standing in front of the cooktop.

He looked up at her with stoic eyes, then nodded his head toward a large metal door off to the side. She followed his lead and grabbed the handle, which pulled out like a latch, and opened it. Suddenly met by a gust of icy cold air, Nell realized that she was staring into the kitchen's walk-in freezer.

And at Saoirse sitting on a stack of giant bags of frozen crinkle cut fries.

"You're going to serve *frozen* French fries?" Nell asked, breaking the silence with a light-hearted chuckle.

Saoirse lifted her chin to look at her, a small smile on her lips and frustration in her eyes. "You followed me in here to ask about my menu?"

"Well, at first I was going to ask you to marry me, but that seems like a bad idea given the history there," Nell joked as she took a seat on a stack of sealed crates next to her. It wobbled beneath her, so she leaned forward to put more of her weight on her feet and prop her elbows on her knees.

"Ha. Ha. Ha," Saoirse replied in a flat monotone. "You're *so* funny."

Nell reached out and touched her shoulder. Her bare skin was prickled with goosebumps and cold to the touch. "Want to get out of the walk-in freezer? You're pretty cold."

Saoirse eyed her for a moment, before sighing and standing. They both walked out, and Nell closed the freezer door behind them. She gestured toward the back door instead and when she opened it, she discovered that it led to a small hallway that connected different shops in the mall. She assumed it was so store owners could take trash in and out without walking past customers, but for now it seemed like a private place to talk.

"It's not much warmer out here," Saoirse commented as she wrapped her arms around herself, rubbing her upper arms.

"It's still March, and you just got out of the freezer," Nell reminded her, even though it certainly felt better out here to her than in the subzero freezer. "It'll warm up soon enough."

They were both quiet for a minute, standing next to each other but not looking at one another. Finally, Saoirse broke the silence.

"I guess I owe you an explanation," she said.

Nell shook her head but continued to stare straight ahead. "You really don't. I mean, it's kind of weird we both dated the same person, but I've seen stranger things."

Saoirse lifted one brow as she looked up at her. "Like what?"

"Like a grown woman running away and hiding in a freezer." Nell leaned back against the wall and kicked one foot up behind her on it. She looked sideways at her and gave a sly smile. "I mean, I've heard of coming out of the closet before...but the freezer?"

Saoirse laughed at that, and her shoulders dropped as some of her tension seemed to ease. "I'm kind of a mess, if you haven't noticed. Relationships aren't easy for me."

Nell didn't say anything, wanting to give her the chance to share more if she wanted to.

"It was just me and my mom for my whole life," Saoirse finally said, her voice quiet and strained. "By the time my mom was diagnosed with ovarian cancer, she was dead four months later. She was gone before I even got my grades back on my last finals in college."

Nell cringed at the sound of pain etched into Saoirse's voice. "I'm so sorry."

"My therapist said that I've been trying to recreate a family in every relationship since, as if I'm trying to do things differently than my mom. Build a new family to avoid the pain of losing mine, of being left completely alone in this world. Or maybe of trying to get it right like my mother never did—build a relationship that was stable. Nothing like my father. But nothing and no one has been quite the right fit to make me feel any better about losing her." Saoirse sighed. "It's kind of pathetic, honestly."

"No, it's not," Nell interjected, shaking her head.

"Nothing about grief is pathetic. I've always thought of it as one of the bravest things someone can do—love so wholly and completely, and then find a way to keep breathing after that person is gone. That's courage. That's resilience."

Saoirse didn't respond to that right away, so Nell continued.

"Listen, I might not fully understand," she began. "I never felt that level of connection to anyone, but particularly a parent. I'm a foster kid, you know? The Winterses adopted me when I was a teenager and are the closest thing I have to loving a parent, but I've never let them fully in either. They asked if I wanted to take their last name and I said no. I wanted to keep my link to...to what? I don't even know. It's not anything that they've ever done—they are amazing—but it's just like that past part of myself doesn't have an access point. To anyone."

"Is that what happened with Abby?" she asked. "Why did you two break up?"

Nell shook her head. "I don't think I ever told that to Abby. She was all lust and excitement—a taboo romance between student and teacher. My first everything, you know? It wasn't much deeper than that. She had her own issues, and I...I was still figuring out who I was, let alone how to let someone in."

"And now?" Saoirse asked.

She tipped her head to the side, looking carefully at Saoirse. "Now what?"

"Do you still not feel that connection with anyone?" she repeated.

Nell didn't respond immediately, but when she did, it was quieter than before. "Maybe. Maybe I'm open to it for the right person. But not as a replacement for anyone I've lost. I am okay with keeping the broken parts of me empty out of respect for those losses—they made me who I am. Everything else I want to fill with someone new who helps me expand my heart in ways that make the broken parts feel much smaller."

"It sounds so simple when you say it that way," Saoirse said, her voice beginning to falter. "But...Nell, I can't promise you anything."

Nell shook her head. "I'm not asking you for anything."

They both stared at one another, neither person speaking. Nell reached out a hand toward Saoirse—a small offering to meet in the middle. Saoirse looked at her hand, unsure, then slipped her fingers between Nell's. She leaned against the wall next to Nell, their hands latched together tightly as they faced one another. There was barely any room between them now, and Nell looked down at Saoirse's perfect pink lips for long enough to feel her chest swell and warm.

"What are we doing?" Saoirse whispered, her eyes fluttering closed as she breathed out.

Nell took a deep breath, trying to reset the moment between them.

"We're going back inside, going to have an incredible opening night, sell a crap ton of green drinks, and then get a good night's sleep because tomorrow we're having brunch with Abby to smooth things over," Nell replied in a matter-of-fact tone that bordered on sarcasm.

Saoirse's eyes flew open. "We're doing *what* tomorrow?"

Nell grinned devilishly. "You already stood her up at the altar. I'm pretty sure you can make it through one brunch. I mean, how much worse can it get?"

"Nell!" Saoirse laughed and shook her head. "Are you insane?"

"Probably." Nell let go of Saoirse's hand and instead

wrapped her arms around her waist and pulled her into her. "But I think you might be, too. Maybe that's why this might actually work."

Her face flushed, and she ducked her chin so that her forehead touched Nell's. "I'm going to need to go back to therapy after all this."

"Highly recommended," Nell agreed with a laugh.

Saoirse pressed her lips to Nell and her arms snaked around Nell's neck, holding her closer. She was soft and timid, and all Nell wanted was to assure her that she wasn't going anywhere in that moment. She was in this.

Whatever the heck *this* was.

EPILOGUE
TWO YEARS LATER

"Do you have the rings?" Heat flushed Saoirse's face as she ran into the small bridal suite on top of the museum curator's office.

"Me?" Mara asked, looking taken aback as she pulled the strap from her bridesmaid's dress up her shoulder. "Was I supposed to have them?"

"Well, then who has them?" Saoirse asked. She could definitely feel the temperature in her cheeks rising to scorching levels as she thought of the possibility of disappointing the bride. "I can't find them anywhere!"

"Oh, I have them!" A little girl with bright blond curls bounced over to them in a rush and held up a velvet ring box. "Both are in here!"

"Noelle, you are a saint," Saoirse exclaimed, taking the box from the young girl that she'd gotten to know over the last few years as Nell's niece. "Where are your parents?"

Nell's brother, Dash, and his wife, Chrissy, had two children, and Noelle was their oldest. She'd been asked to be the flower girl at today's ceremony.

"They're already sitting down," Noelle said. "They said they were ready to celebrate love."

Saoirse understood that to mean that they'd already been seated in the museum where the wedding procession had been set up and she was all on her own to figure this out.

Despite the last minute details, she was excited for the wedding. It had taken some coordination to get fifty chairs and an arch into the center of the Bentley Museum at the University of Michigan's Spectrum Center, but all of it was worth it to throw the queer wedding of the bride's dreams.

In celebration of when they'd met, the wedding was themed in white and green, and the entire aisle was going to be coated with four-leaf clovers laid down by the flower girl instead of the traditional rose petals.

"Okay, hold on to those rings," she told Noelle, trying to make a mental list of what else needed to be done. "We can't lose them before the wedding."

Noelle tucked them into the small velvet pouch tied around her wrist. "I know. I've got my eyes on them the whole time. I promise, Aunt Saoirse."

Saoirse smiled at the young girl, her heart swelling at the term of endearment. It was weird to be an aunt, but it felt more natural than she'd expected. Meeting Nell and blending into her family had been mostly seamless, and then falling in love with her family hadn't been a difficult feat at all.

"She's ready!" the maid of honor called out as she walked into the bridal suite from the bathroom off the side. "Are you guys ready to see the bride?"

Everyone in the room, including the makeup artist and photographer, clapped and cheered.

"Did I miss it?" Nell said as she slid in next to Saoirse

and wrapped her arms around Saoirse's waist, placing a soft kiss against her cheek.

She looked incredible in her gray suit with a green vest underneath that celebrated the St. Patrick's Day holiday and the theme of the wedding—*Kiss Me, I'm marrying an Irish Woman*!

Saoirse shook her head, returning her girlfriend's kiss. "No. She's coming now!"

Abby walked out in a fanfare of bright white lace and a long train veil with intricate lace four-leaf clovers designed into it. "Well, what do you guys think?"

The room burst into applause and *awwwws*. It truly was a beautiful look, and despite the fact that Saoirse wasn't the bride, she could really appreciate her friend's beauty.

"Oh my gosh, you look amazing!" Saoirse exclaimed. "Benny is the luckiest woman!"

Nell clapped and said the same thing, while every bridesmaid and member of the wedding party shouted similar sentiments. Saoirse was so happy for Abby, because despite how difficult their history had been, she only wanted the best for her.

Leaving Abby at the altar had been the right choice, but not necessarily done in the right way or the kindest. She knew that now, and maybe a few more years of therapy was to thank for that, or maybe it was Nell's consistent and steadfast love over the last two years. Either way, Saoirse felt like a different version of herself—a stronger version. She loved who she was, but she was damn excited to see who she was becoming and felt sure that her mother would have been too, if only she could see her now.

"I would never have met Benny without the two of you," Abby said as she walked over and grabbed both Saoirse's and Nell's hands—one in each. "I know we have our history, but, you guys are an inspiration for what I want one day."

Nell laughed. "Even though we're not married and you're about to be?"

Abby grinned and waved her hand, as if it wasn't relevant. "In my mind, you already are."

"Right?" Saoirse blushed as she leaned back enough to kiss Nell one more time. "It definitely feels like we're an old married couple."

When they'd had brunch two years ago with Abby after that fateful St. Patrick's Day spat, they'd all been able to smooth things out, including forgiving each other for everything that had transpired. What they hadn't expected, however, was for Abby to run into the hostess at the restaurant where they had eaten and fall head over heels in love with her. She and Benny had been going strong since that day, and Saoirse was beyond excited to celebrate their wedding today.

Being a bridesmaid at her ex-fiancée's wedding certainly wasn't something she'd ever thought might happen, but it all felt pretty normal now. Or maybe they had just normalized it for themselves because this was their life.

Everyone spent a few more minutes fawning over Abby's dress before Saoirse and Nell escaped out into the hallway to head down to the museum's main corridor and inspect everything was set up and ready.

"Is this weird for you?" Nell asked her as they walked down the aisle of empty chairs. A few guests were randomly seated throughout, but most people had not arrived yet.

Saoirse shook her head. "No. Why?"

"I mean, walking down the aisle of your ex-fiancée's wedding with your never-fiancée girlfriend?" Nell laughed lightly and shook her head. "You have to admit, it's a tad strange."

"When you say it like that, sure," Saoirse agreed, chuckling.

They paused at the bottom of the aisle when no one was watching and Nell wrapped her arms around Saoirse's waist and placed a soft kiss on her lips. She leaned into it, her arms wrapping around Nell's neck and pulling her closer.

"Never?" Saoirse whispered.

Nell frowned. "Never what?"

"You said your *never-fiancée*," Saoirse repeated, kissing her again. "Did you really mean that?"

"Are you asking me to marry you, Sersh?" Nell kidded, letting her mouth travel down to Saoirse's neck and kissing her way to her collarbone. "I told you if you ever wanted to actually lock me down, you'd have to get on one knee and ask me yourself."

"I didn't say *that* specifically," Saoirse countered, feeling flustered. It wasn't that she wanted to get married—her three failed engagements were enough to show that that wasn't of interest to her. But something about the woman she loved saying *never* struck her in a way that she hadn't expected.

Was that something she wanted one day?

"I just meant, like...why say *never*?" Saoirse shrugged. "It just seems very final."

Nell laughed and bit down on her tongue, sliding it against her bottom lip in the way that always made Saoirse's core tighten with excitement. "You're going to have to woo me if that's what you want one day, baby."

Saoirse grinned, batting her lashes at Nell in a teasing manner. "I'm not saying *today*."

"Babe, I love you," Nell repeated, kissing her jawline

before finding her mouth again. "But there's nothing about you and I that isn't final. I don't need a piece of paper with the courts to prove that."

Her heart pounded in her chest, but it wasn't the fearful anxiety type of pounding she'd felt each time she'd been steps away from the altar before. Instead, it was the type of beating that made her feel whole and seen, and like this was exactly where she'd always been meant to be.

"I'm definitely not saying I'm marrying you one day, Nell," Saoirse repeated. "Just to be clear."

"Loud and clear since day one," Nell confirmed. She took her hand and intertwined her fingers with hers. "Come on. We've got to help Abby actually make it down the aisle this time."

Saoirse laughed. "Never thought I'd be here to see that happen."

"I love you, Sersh."

She smiled. "Love you, too, Nell. Happy St. Patrick's Day...again."

SUBSCRIBE TO SARAH'S NEWSLETTER!

For more news on upcoming releases, giveaways, freebies, and exclusive excerpts, make sure to join Sarah's newsletter sent out 1-2x/month!

>> JOIN HERE <<

Want Alerts on $0.99 Sales for Sarah's Books?
Follow Sarah Robinson on Bookbub for deal alerts when any of her novels go on sale for limited times!

>> JOIN HERE <<

Keep reading for a short excerpt from two other novels!

EXCERPT FROM MALL I WANT FOR CHRISTMAS IS YOU

A HOLIDAY ROMANCE

CHAPTER ONE

DASH

HO HO HORRIBLE.

Dash Winters took one look at the frayed velvet red suit that the manager of Yule Heights Shopping Mall was handing him. "It's...um...it's very large."

"Oh, right." The manager turned around and reached into a metal cabinet and pulled out two yellowed pillows without any pillowcases. It was clear that they'd been white once upon a time, but now...not so much.

He grimaced at the mystery stains as the manager also handed him a thick Velcro belt. Honestly, the poor man couldn't have been older than Dash's foster father, but he spoke with a weariness that sounded ancient. "Here. Put the pillow against your stomach and wrap the band around you so it stays put. You'll look as holly jolly as any other mall Santa out there."

"Great." Dash tucked the outfit and pillow under one muscled arm and sidestepped a leak of some mystery liquid from the paneled ceiling. "So, when do I start?"

The harried manager tossed a fake white, curly beard at

Dash which he barely caught in time. "What do you mean? You start now."

"Like *now* now?" Dash had only come in for an interview, but he hadn't expected to get the job immediately. Not that he'd thought competition for mall Santa was all that intense. Especially considering his foster mother had called ahead as city councilwoman to pave the way for him.

He tucked that embarrassing thought away.

"There is already a line of kids waiting, and the Santa we've used the last few years was just arrested for driving under the influence," the manager sat down in his desk chair with a heavy thud. "I can't explain to a bunch of children that Santa drank too much milk with his cookies. So, you're it, kid."

Dash bristled slightly at the term *kid*. He was, after all, twenty-eight years old. Though he knew he had a youthful look to him, it still hit a sore spot. Probably because he had returned to living in his childhood bedroom in his foster parent's house and was now employed full-time—at least for the next twenty-five days—as a mall Santa as a favor to his mother. Despite the unfortunate turn of events his life had taken, he was trying to look at the bright side. This was all for a purpose, and, in the end, it would be worth it.

At least, that's what he hoped.

"Thanks," he replied, pulling the chord for the beard around his neck and letting it hang down like a necklace. "Is there a place I should change?"

The manager didn't even glance up from the computer he was now furiously typing away on. "The employee bathroom is at the end of the hall. The door next to the dumpsters."

Of course it was.

Dash nodded and headed out of the small office that

looked more like a converted storage closet. It had absolutely no windows and was off a concrete hallway that ran the length of the mall behind the stores. Random containers or bags of garbage were sitting outside metal doors that were marked with a store's name—most of which he recognized— but then the rest of the hallway was just empty. The off-putting lights above him was missing several bulbs and there was a buzzing sound come from a flickering bulb behind him.

He'd spent most of the last decade in Yule Heights, Michigan, after being placed with his foster parents—who he now considered just his parents—at age sixteen. He'd spent many Friday and Saturday nights loitering around this mall, but it had never occurred to him that there was an intricate behind-the-scenes set up connecting all the stores together and allowing a clear path to the garbage or parking lot without being seen by customers.

The closer he got to his destination, the stronger the smell of garbage was. A small *employee restroom* sign was hanging crookedly from one nail on the back of a door at the end of the hall, and Dash quickly made his way inside and locked it behind him after he switched on the lights.

He turned back around and surveyed the situation. The room was small enough that if he wanted to sit on the toilet and wash his hands at the same time, he certainly could. Dash hung the suit up on the back of the door, praying the rusty hook would hold. The walls were covered in crude drawings, graffiti, and flyers to someone's upcoming garage concert. He smiled slightly when he read the sloppy handwriting on the cracked mirror that said *don't hate me because I'm beautiful, hate me because I fucked your dad.* Someone else had written in another color and handwriting underneath, *go home, mom, you're drunk.*

Okay, so it wasn't all bad.

Dash made quick work of climbing out of his jeans and the ugly Christmas sweater with at least one hundred reindeer on it his mom had insisted he wear stating that it would *nail the spirit of the interview.* To be fair, she'd been right. The manager had taken one look at him and hired him on the spot.

The red pants for the Santa suit hung loosely around his legs, despite the fact that he had generally pretty thick thighs and calves. He spent one to two hours a day working out at the Planet Fitness on the other side of the mall since he didn't have much else to do with his time these days.

Another part of the reason his mother had demanded he get a job and get out of the house.

His phone started buzzing from the pocket of his discarded jeans. He fished it out and hit the answer button, accepting the video call from his older foster sister, Nell, as he propped the phone up on the bathroom sink.

"Oh, God." Nell immediately groaned through the phone. Her bright purple hair was tossed over her shoulder and he could tell from the background behind her that she was in her small kitchen apartment. She had an unusual obsession with roosters and her kitchen was decked out in cock-a-doodle-doos. "Where the hell are you? And why are you naked?"

"I have pants on." He pointed the camera down to show his bright red pants. "I'm trying to strap these pillows to my waist."

Her face scrunched up with even more confusion. "You're what?"

Dash held up his Santa hat to remind her.

Nell laughed, then took a bite of something off a large

spoon from her stove. "I forgot you were doing that. Lilian really wasn't kidding, was she?"

"Mom doesn't have a sense of humor, but she tries," Dash replied, finally getting the two pillows anchored to his stomach. He pulled the jacket overtop and attempted to button it up. "She's been asking if you're coming for Christmas Eve dinner, by the way."

"I know." Nell sighed and leaned down, propping herself up on her elbows in front of the camera. "I'm thinking about it."

"Come on, Nell. You know how much it would mean to her. Plus, none of us know what's going on with your life lately. You're like a vault." Dash pulled on the hat and adjusted his fake beard. He put out his hands in triumph. "There. Do I look like Saint Nick?"

Nell grinned and shook her head. "I'm going to need to come down to the mall sometime soon to watch you in action."

"You wouldn't dare," he threatened. "Gotta go, Nell. Christmas is calling."

She gave a quick wave and then disappeared from the screen. Dash grabbed his phone and tucked it into the waist-band on his pants since he couldn't seem to find a pocket. Previous girlfriends had always complained about pants without pockets, but it wasn't until this moment that he realized how truly irritating that was.

Dash quickly tucked his previous clothes in an old grocery store bag and then left for the center of the mall. He was familiar with the Santa's Village set that was constructed in the mall's main hallway every winter, though he'd never actually participated in it before. Hell, he'd never done any sort of Santa or Christmas-themed activity until he'd moved in with the Winters. After they'd adopted him, he began to follow along with their Christmas traditions, of which there were many. The Winters did not play around when it came to holiday spirit. Their house was professional decorated, appropriately fake-snowed, and lit up bright enough to be seen the next county over.

"Santa!"

The moment Dash stepped out into the mall walkway, several little kids waved to him from behind ropes. His eyes widened as he tried to count how many children were in line, but he couldn't even see the end.

Dash waved to the crowd as a hefty, sweaty man wearing a too-tight elf costume came rushing toward him. "Uh, hello?"

"It's about time," the elf growled, grabbing the grocery bag from his hand and tossing it behind some fake presents. "Get up in your chair. Time is money, and Santa has a quota."

"He does?" Dash furrowed his brow. He was beginning to realize he should probably have asked more questions about the job to the other guy. "Oh, okay. I'll get started. What's your name?"

"Donner," the grumpy elf replied, speaking through a clenched smile that was clearly for show. "Now, let's go. I bring the kids to you, they tell you what they want. You promise them whatever they're asking for, hand them a little wrapped trinket, snap a picture for mom, and, lather, rinse, repeat."

Dash took his seat in the large red and gold throne, then waved a white-gloved hand at the line of children. Donner went to the front of the line and invited the first kid and her mother up to meet him in a sing-song voice that was clearly not his natural aggravated tone.

"Well, ho, ho, ho, young one," Dash greeted the little girl

as he helped her up onto his knee. "And what are you asking Santa for Christmas this year?"

"I want a unicorn. But it has to be rainbow." She began describing the intricate details of her unicorn dream and Dash just nodded along, chuckling. He promised her that he would see what he could do, and then they smiled for the formal photographer and for the mom who snapped a few cell phone pictures.

Next up was a slightly older boy, though he couldn't have been more than eight years old. Dash encouraged him to come on up, but the kid's feet were like concrete and he refused to move. His mother was pushing him forward, whispering harshly in his ear to *go*.

"Ho, ho, ho! Merry Christmas!" Dash greeted him once he was close enough.

The boy burst into tears and took off at a run. The mother apologized profusely and then went to chase after him.

"Rough start, Klaus." Donner shook his head and then turned a wide smile back to the crowd. "Next!"

An hour went by so fast, he hadn't even realized that he wasn't anywhere near the end of the line yet. In fact, it seemed like the line was just getting longer. Given that it was the middle of the day on a Saturday in early December, this wasn't exactly shocking.

It was, however, exhausting.

Dash enjoyed chatting with the kids about their Christmas wishes and he'd heard everything from wanting the latest Xbox to wanting parents reunited after a divorce. Despite his enjoyment, children were an incredible amount of energy. As a single man with no kids in his current life, he hadn't been fully prepared for both the volume and stickiness of this younger generation.

"Can I take a quick five?" Dash asked his elf helper between children. He glanced down at the wet candy cane stuck to his glove. "I just need to get some water. And maybe wash my hands."

Donner nodded and pulled the rope across the front of the line. "Santa's needed in his workshop! He'll be back in five minutes!"

There were a few groans from the families in line, but Dash tried not to feel guilty. He was technically only getting paid thirteen dollars an hour for this job, and he already needed a nap.

He'd move as quickly as possible, but there was no way in hell he was going back to that employee restroom by the dumpster.

Ignoring the awkward stares, Dash made his way—in full Santa gear—to the customer's bathroom off the main corridor. There was a short line of men waiting, but they were moving much quicker than the extensive line winding its way out of the ladies' room next door.

"Uh, you can go ahead of me, Santa," a young man stepped aside in line and offered him his spot.

He considered it for a moment, but he was in a rush. "Thanks, man."

"No problem. I don't want to be on your naughty list!" The young man was laughing now, and Dash rolled his eyes, but cut in front of him anyway.

After a quick visit to a stall, Dash found himself at the wide, multi-person sink trying to scrub off the candy cane now glued to his glove. A young boy came up to the sink next to him and began washing his hands, but his gaze was glued to Dash's reflection in the mirror before them.

Dash gave him a polite smile, then returned to his task.

The young boy pushed up on his tiptoes in order to turn

off the faucet. He paused and turned to face Dash. "Are you...are you Santa?"

He glanced down to see bright green eyes peeking out at him from under a thick mop of shaggy brown hair hanging low on the boy's forehead. "What?"

"Are you...um, are you Santa?"

Dash pulled his glove back on after he'd gotten off as much of the candy cane remnants off as possible. He smiled at the boy and deepened his voice. "I am. Merry Christmas!"

"My mom said we could come see you, but she's working all day," the young boy explained. "Can I tell you what I want for Christmas even though we're in a bathroom?"

Another man walked past them to the open sink, side-eyeing him. Dash cleared his throat and then got down on one knee. "Sure, kid. What's your name?"

"I'm Rudy." The boy beamed and straightened, standing taller. "Last year, you got me a model-making kit. I made a replica of the Eiffel Tower."

"That's pretty cool," Dash replied, chuckling and giving his best *ho ho ho* in the throaty laugh. "How'd it turn out?"

"Great! I love it! I still play with it," Rudy confessed. He was fidgeting with his hands now. "But, this year, can I ask for something for my mom?"

Dash tilted his head to the side. He smiled at the sweet concern on the boy's face. "Well, sure. Moms need Christmas gifts, too."

Rudy nodded. "I made her a picture with my teacher, too."

"Great job," Dash replied.

The boy stepped a little closer and lowered his voice slightly. "I was hoping you could teach my mom how to drive a sleigh."

He paused, considering the strange request. "You want me to teach your mom how to drive a sleigh?"

"She's *terrible* at driving," Rudy continued. "And she said that's why we don't have a car. But sleighs are harder to drive than cars, right? So, maybe if she learns how to drive a sleigh, then she can drive a car!"

"That is...well, that is some sound logic, son," Dash said with a laugh. "I can see this is important to you."

"It is," Rudy agreed. "I don't want to keep taking the bus everywhere. It's so smelly, and we have to get up so early to make it across town for her shift on weekends. I know she says it's fine, but I can tell she hates it, too."

Dash felt a thump in his chest as he pictured this little boy on a bus every weekend accompanying his mom to work. He certainly wasn't a stranger to buses. Hell, he'd spent most of his childhood using that as his sole means of transportation. Since finding the Winters, however, his life had changed dramatically. He had been gifted a car that he loved and refused to get rid of even years later when it had certainly seen better days. "Uh, so...where's your mom, kid?"

"I'll bring you to her!" Rudy grabbed his gloved hand and started pulling him toward the door. "Then you can tell her in person!"

Dash allowed himself to be led away, trying to figure out how he'd explain to Donner that he was teaching someone to drive a sleigh on his short bathroom break.

Well, won't that be awkward.

Live on All Retailers:

https://booksbysarahrobinson.com/books/mall-i-want-for-christmas-is-you/

EXCERPT FROM MISADVENTURES IN THE CAGE

A MISADVENTURES ROMANCE

CHAPTER ONE

"OH MY GOD...JOSIE? JOSIE GRAY?" A young African American woman with short black hair and a vibrantly metallic dress on sidled up to her at the bar. "Can I please get a picture with you?"

Josie shot back the glass of tequila and then sucked on the lime, hissing as it hit her stomach hard. She was already four shots in and each one was helping her forget the giant rejection letter she was carrying around in her purse.

We regret to inform you that the position of sous chef is no longer available blah blah blah.

She got the point. She was never going to be a chef. Every job application she'd sent in over the last year had been turned down.

Not that she was even allowed to be one anyway.

"Sure," she replied, finally turning to the woman and putting on her best fake smile.

The woman held up her iPhone, turning the camera around to face them and put on her best duck face as she posed for the camera next to Josie.

Josie just smiled and then turned back to the bar as soon as the photo was done.

"Another one," she indicated to the bartender, but when she lifted her hand to motion, she knocked over her glass. Thankfully, it didn't shatter, but it made a loud ass noise as it clattered against the bar.

The bartender shook his head, casting her a pitying look. God, she hated that. "Miss Gray, I think you've had enough. Why don't I call you a cab?"

"No," she sighed loudly. Admittedly, she was getting tired and had probably had enough. Plus, she couldn't really afford TMZ to find her and write an article about how the reality television star was wasted and falling all over herself at a local bar. Hell, it was the entire reason she'd come to this place off the strip to begin with—anonymity. So much for that. "I'll order a Lyft. Thank you, though."

She paid her check and then pulled out her phone, ordering a ride through the ride share app. Honestly, she wasn't normally like this. She didn't regularly go get drunk by herself at a bar off the Las Vegas strip in a seedy part of town.

Hell, this entire town was a seedy part of town depending on how you looked at it.

She'd spent her entire life living in Las Vegas though, so it was home to her. She was comfortable with its antics and qualms. Something about it...she could handle. At least, that's what she told herself.

Pulling her sweater up around her shoulders, she grabbed her purse and decided to wait for her Lyft out front. She could really use the still, night air to sober up before getting in a lurching car ride. God forbid she puke in the back of someone else's car.

She debated canceling the Lyft and just calling her

driver, but then he would tell her brother where she'd been and she'd never hear the end of it. No, she needed the time off the clock and away from the freaking cameras.

"Hey, Miss," a voice called out to her as she stood on the front steps of the bar trying to take some deep breaths. "You left this on the bar."

She turned to see an older gentleman, maybe twenty years her senior, approaching her. He was holding a tube of lipstick. She didn't recognize it and it certainly wasn't hers. She never wore lipstick.

She shook her head. "That's not mine."

"Are you sure?" He frowned, then glanced back up at her. "I bet it would look real pretty on your chocolate skin."

Josie pulled her sweater tighter around her, hoping the Lyft decided to show up sooner rather than later. "It's not mine," she repeated.

"Why don't you try it on?" he insisted. "Let's just test it out."

"No." She moved away from him, but he approached her faster.

"Just try it on, sweet thing." He grabbed her wrist and twisted it, yanking her backward. "I just want to see how it looks on ya."

"Let go of me!" she yelled, struggling to free her arm from his grasps.

"Don't be such an uppity little bitch," the older man said, squeezing her wrist tighter and tighter until she cried out in pain. "I've seen you on TV before."

"Hey!" A fist came out of nowhere and landed squarely against the older man's jaw.

He staggered back, releasing Josie's wrist and clutching his bruising face. "What the hell?"

"The lady said let go," the owner of the fist—a tall, buff

young man who looked like a brick wall stuffed in a suit—instructed her attacker. "I suggest you listen to women when they talk. I'd also suggest you leave and not come back. Now."

The older man scurried away like a dog with his tail between his legs. She wasn't sorry to see him go.

The newcomer turned back to her, concern etched on his features as his brows furrowed. "Are you okay?"

"I...I think so?" She got back up to her feet and examined her wrist, wincing at the pain.

He noticed her expression right away. "We need to get you to a hospital."

"No way," she opposed the idea right away. "I'm not spending all night in a hospital room when I know it's not broken. It just needs some ice probably."

Plus, she couldn't afford the fall out from the media over yet another family scandal. It was bad enough that her entire family was on a reality television show thanks to her brother's career that chronicled her every move, but knowing that any little thing she did could be used as fodder for an episode was a nightmare waiting to happen.

"See, I can still move it?" She gingerly moved her wrist.

A small smirk played across his lips and she couldn't help but notice a slight Irish accent to his words. "Useful."

"Thank you for your help," she stammered, trying to find something to say to this incredibly gorgeous man who'd just rode in like Prince Charming and saved her life. "I'll just go find my Lyft now."

"What's your name?" he asked, seeming to ignore everything she just said.

"Josie." It was a nice change of pace to run into someone who didn't know who she was. Although, that wasn't very unusual with men because they weren't really the target demographic for her family's show.

He nodded. "I'm Callan."

"Nice to meet you, Callan." She started to walk away again, but he interrupted her again.

"Need a ride home?" he asked, motioning to his car parked against the curb. Of course, it had to be a freaking Range Rover. She wondered who the hell was this guy. It certainly wasn't unusual in Las Vegas to run in to celebrities, but she didn't recognize him...although something about his face...he did look familiar.

She glanced down at her phone and checked her Lyft app. Her driver was still thirteen minutes away. *What the hell?* She canceled the ride. "Sure? Why not."

A ride with a life-saving, potential celebrity sounded safer anyway than with a total stranger vetted only by an app. At least, that's the story she was going to tell herself to convince herself to get into the car with this drop dead handsome man. And when she said drop dead handsome, she meant it. The dude was gawking-worthy. Chiseled muscles on every inch of his body that she could see. Long, brown wavy hair tied back in a pony tail, and blue eyes that made her knees feel like they were made of jello.

"Is this your car?" she asked, motioning to the Range Rover.

He nodded and opened the passenger door for her. "Hop in."

"Hold on. One second." She walked around to the front of the car and took a picture of the car and license plate and sent it off in a quick text to her best friend, Emily.

"Did you just take a picture of my license plate?" he asked, one brow raised as he watched her.

"And texted it to my friend," she confirmed, waltzing past him and climbing into the passenger seat of the car.

He chuckled, leaning against the door frame. "Can I ask why?"

"In case you murder me, obviously." She turned to face him, giving him a deadpan expression like it was the most obvious thing ever. Honestly, it was. Her mother had taught her that trick years ago, and you learn a thing or two growing up in Las Vegas. Men are a lot less likely to act nefariously when they know they're being held accountable by an anonymous third party.

A grin spread wide across his face and it only made his beautiful features all the more glorious. "Smart lady." He closed her car door and she watched as he walked around the car and then climbed into the driver's seat. "Where to, Ms. Precaution?"

Maybe it was the tequila talking, or maybe it was the fact that he was daring her to throw caution to the wind, or maybe she was just fed up with the monotony of her life and wanted to throw a wrench at things. She wasn't sure what made the next words come out of her mouth. All she knew was that she said them and she didn't want to take them back...and thank God, she didn't.

"Take me to your place."

Live on All Retailers:
booksbysarahrobinson.com/books/misadventures-in-the-cage/

ABOUT THE AUTHOR

Sarah Robinson first started her writing career as a published poet in high school, and then continued in college, winning several poetry awards and being published in multiple local literary journals.

Never expecting to make a career of it, a freelance writing Craigslist job accidentally introduced her to the world of book publishing. Lengthening her writing from poetry to novels, Robinson published her first book through a small press publisher, before moving into self-publishing, and then finally accepting a contract from Penguin Random House two years later. She continues to publish both traditionally and indie with over 18+ novels to her name with publishers like Penguin, Waterhouse Press, Hachette, and more. She has achieved awards and accolades including 2021 Vivian Award Finalist, Top 10 iBooks Bestseller, Top

25 Amazon Kindle Bestseller, and Top 5 Barnes & Noble Bestseller. She has been published in three languages.

In her personal life, Sarah Robinson is happily married to the gentle giant of her dreams and the duo recently welcomed to the world their first baby, Norah Grace. They have a home full of love, snuggly pets, and are happily living in Arlington, Virginia.

Subscribe to her newsletter for more regular information.

Did You Enjoy This Novella? Leave a Review!

You can help the author by **leaving a review**! Reviews on the online book retailer where you purchased this novella help the author so much!

I Want To Do More! How Else Can I Help?

If you want to get even more involved and help the author, you can follow Sarah on social media and interact online! You can join Sarah's Facebook Reader Group (Robinson's Ramblings) and/or her newsletter (here)! You can also follow any of her social media sites below!

Follow the Author on Social Media

booksbysarahrobinson.com
subscribepage.com/sarahrobinsonnewsletter
facebook.com/booksbysarahrobinson
twitter.com/booksby_sarah

goodreads.com/booksbysarahrobinson
instagram.com/booksbysarahrobinson

ALSO BY SARAH ROBINSON

The Photographer Trilogy

(*Romantic Suspense*)

Tainted Bodies

Tainted Pictures

Untainted

Forbidden Rockers Series

(*Rockstar Romances*)

Logan's Story: A Prequel Novella

Her Forbidden Rockstar

Rocker Christmas: A Logan & Caroline Holiday Novella

Kavanagh Legends Series

(*MMA Fighter Standalone Romances*)

Breaking a Legend

Saving a Legend

Becoming a Legend

Chasing a Legend

Kavanagh Christmas

Nudes Series

(*Hollywood Standalone Romances*)

NUDES

BARE

SHEER

At the Mall Series

(*Romantic Comedy Shorts*)

Mall I Want for Christmas is You

Mall You Need is Love

Mall Out of Luck

More coming soon...

Heart Lake Series

(*Small Town Romances*)

Dreaming of a Heart Lake Christmas (Coming September 2022)

Standalone Novels

Not a Hero: A Bad Boy Marine Romance

Misadventures in the Cage

One Night Stand Serial

Second Shot of Whiskey

Women's Fiction

Every Last Drop

More books and series by Sarah Robinson are coming soon, check her website for the latest news and releases, or subscribe to her newsletter to never miss one!

Made in the USA
Coppell, TX
19 March 2022